W9-CEW-239

First edition for the United States published in 1991 by
Barron's Educational Series, Inc.

First published in 1991 by Simon and Schuster Young Books,
Simon and Schuster Limited, England.

Text copyright © Ken Adams 1991
Illustrations copyright © Val Biro 1991

All rights reserved.
No part of this book may be reproduced in any form,
by photostat, microfilm, xerography, or any other means,
or incorporated into any information retrieval system,
electronic or mechanical, without the written permission
of the copyright owner.

All inquiries should be addressed to:
Barron's Educational Series, Inc.
250 Wireless Boulevard
Hauppauge, New York 11788

Library of Congress Catalog Card No. 91-9174

International Standard Book No. 0-8120-6249-3

Library of Congress Cataloging-in-Publication Data

Adams, Ken.
    When I was your age / by Ken Adams ; illustrated by Val Bira.
      p.   cm.
    Summary: A grandfather exaggerates his stories to his young
grandson about how much he ate when he himself was a child,
how far he walked, and other aspects of his life then.
    ISBN 0-8120-6249-3
    [1. Grandfathers—Fiction.   2. Tall tales.]
I. Biro, Val, 1921– ill. II. Title.
P27. A2172Wh 1991 91-9174 CIP
[E]—dc20

PRINTED IN BELGIUM
1 2 3 4   9 8 7 6 5 4 3 2 1

When I Was Your Age

by Ken Adams
illustrated by Val Biro

BARRON'S

NEW YORK

On Monday, Grandpa came to stay.
He helped Sammy clear the table after lunch.

"I wish Mom wouldn't keep giving me jobs,"
said Sammy. "I had to make my bed
this morning, too."

"When I was your age," said Grandpa . . .

"I had to make all
the beds in the house,

wash every floor and clean all the windows,
inside and out, all before school.
That's how hard I had to work."

"I don't think so," said Sammy.

Later, Sammy emptied his money box onto the kitchen table.

"I've got two dollars left from my birthday money," he said, "and one dollar of my allowance to come. I can buy something good with all that."

"When I was your age," said Grandpa . . .

"I was so rich that for my mother's birthday I bought her a new car, one hundred beautiful dresses, and a castle, with just half of one week's allowance.
That's how rich I was."

"I don't think so," said Sammy.

On Tuesday, Sammy wasn't feeling hungry at supper time.

"I had three helpings of spaghetti for lunch today," he said. "I'm still full."

"When I was your age," said Grandpa . . .

"I used to eat six bowls of cereal, twenty sausages, ten slices of bacon with fifteen fried eggs, and eleven pieces of toast, and drink three glasses of milk, just for breakfast. That's how good I was at eating."

"I don't think so," said Sammy.

Grandpa helped Sammy get ready for bed that night.

"I need a bigger pair of shoes," said Sammy.
"These are hurting my feet."

"When I was your age," said Grandpa . . .

"my shoes were so big that
when I took them off at night
the toes stuck out of the window
and reached right across the street.
That's how big my shoes were."

"I don't think so," said Sammy.

On Wednesday, Sammy played
for the school soccer team.
"I scored the winning goal,"
he told Grandpa. "I got the
Man of the Match award."

"When I was your age,"
said Grandpa . . .

"I was the only one on the school team.
I played defense, offense, and goalkeeper,
and I won all the matches twenty-five to zero.
That's how good I was at soccer."

"I don't think so," said Sammy.

On Thursday, Grandpa picked Sammy up at school.

"Oh, I am tired," said Sammy. "It's such a long walk home after a hard day's work."

"When I was your age," said Grandpa . . .

"I had to get up in the middle of the night,
walk fifty miles to school, through a crocodile-infested
swamp, and over the highest mountain in the country,
carrying my school books and my little sister on my back.
That's how good I was at walking."

"I don't think so," said Sammy.

That night, Sammy made himself
a sandwich for supper.

"I can't unscrew the top of this jam
jar," he said. "I wish I were stronger."

"When I was your age,"
said Grandpa . . .

"I was so strong that I used to bend a lamp-post to read my comic book better, and wrestle fifteen gorillas with one arm tied behind my back, and still win easily. That's how strong I was."

"I don't think so," said Sammy.

Sammy was glad when school was over on Friday.

"I couldn't do my arithmetic today," he said. "But my teacher says I could do better if I tried hard."

"When I was your age," said Grandpa . . .

"I was so smart I could read my books with one eye closed and balancing on my head. At the same time I juggled sixteen cups and saucers with my toes and told the teacher the answers to all the arithmetic problems she couldn't do. That's how smart I was."

"I don't think so," said Sammy.

Later, Sammy played in the garden.

"Look at me!" he called.
"I've climbed to the top of the apple tree.
Right to the very highest branch."

"When I was your age," said Grandpa . . .

"I used to climb a skyscraper before breakfast, the Eiffel Tower before dinner, and Mount Everest before bedtime.

That's how good
I was at climbing."

"I don't think so,"
said Sammy.

On Saturday, Sammy
got out his new racing bike.

"If you need anything at the
store," he told Grandpa, "I can
get it really quickly on this."

"When I was your age,"
said Grandpa . . .

"I only had a rusty old bike, but in one morning I rode it to the North Pole and back . . .

Then I rode across the Sahara Desert,
won a race against a cheetah, and
got back before dinner time.
That's how good I was on my bicycle."

"I don't think so," said Sammy.

Sunday was Grandpa's last day. Sammy came home hot and tired after playing with his friends.

"I'm hungry," said Sammy.
"When will lunch be ready?"

"It's ready now," said Grandpa.
"When I was your age I was famous for my lunches. Now I make the best lunch in the whole world."

"Yes," said Sammy. "I think so!"